Polly's Fabulous Pet Palace

Written by Pamela Jane
Illustrated by MADA Design, Inc.

Manufactured and printed in the United States of America.
ISBN-13: 978-0-696-23187-2
ISBN-10: 0-696-23187-5

We welcome your comments and suggestions.
Write to us at: Meredith Books, Children's Books,
1716 Locust St., Des Moines, IA 50309-3023.
Visit us online at: meredithbooks.com

Meredith₀ Books
Des Moines, Iowa

Super Saturday was only a week away, and the whole town would be turning out for parades, picnics, and parties.

Polly called her pals together for a secret powwow at the mall.

"Listen, everyone." she said. "There will be a huge crowd here on Super Saturday. The timing is perfect for the opening of Polly's Fabulous Pet Palace!"

Kicker curiously poked his head out of Rick's shirt pocket.

"Sweet!" said Shani. "We can showcase our new line of pet jewelry!"

"And the pet playground with the puppy pool!" added Lea.

"Don't forget the pet makeover parlor," Lila added. "Cupcake is so ready for a new look!"

"Totally," said Polly. "But we need a really fabulicious plan for the opening—something to get everyone's attention!"

Samuel poked his head around the corner. "Might I suggest a doggie tea party?" he asked.

Polly laughed. "Something tells me Ollie isn't crazy about tea."

"Sugar, cupcakes, spice, and tea. I love the boys, and the boys love me!" squawked Shani's parrot Rainbow.

Shani giggled. "I've been teaching Rainbow to recite jump rope rhymes. Sometimes he makes up his own."

"That's it!" cried Polly.

"It, fit, I won't quit!" said Rainbow, winking at Polly.

"Great," said Polly, "because we're going to put on a pet talent show!"

"Cool! I'll teach Rainbow a new jump rope rhyme," said Shani. "That will bring in the crowds!"

"My new monkey Hopscotch can swing upside down from the jungle gym by his tail," said Lea.

"Kicker can race on his wheel," said Rick. "He's the fastest hamster ever!"

"And I'll teach Ollie to jump through a hoop," said Polly.

Ollie wagged his tail. "Woof!" "We could have a picnic too," Lea suggested.

Shani shook her head. "No picnics!" she said. "Rainbow goes totally wild when he sees food, especially grapes."

"Grape, grape, big fat ape!" sang Rainbow. Everyone laughed.

"OK," said Polly, "pet show first, parties and picnics later!"
"Way to go, Polly!" said Lila. "It's the ultimate perfect plan!"
Polly grinned. "Perfect planning is the key!"

Beth and her pals, Evie and Tori, peeked around the corner.

"Another perfect Polly plan," whispered Evie.

Beth narrowed her eyes. "What I need is a perfect plot to turn Polly's fabulous plan into a fabulous flop!"

Beth's dog Snarls growled. "GRRRRRRR."

"Good boy, Snarls!" said Beth. "When I put my plan into action, you'll be top dog, and I'll be the Number One cool girl in school!"

Polly and her pals arrived at Polly's Fabulous Pet Palace early Saturday morning. "Wow, this stuff is rockin'!" cried Shani.

All the animals were groomed and looking their best. Kicker had a tiny baseball cap to match Rick's, Ollie had a glittering new collar, and Lila and Cupcake were wearing matching sweaters.

"Let's hang up our new sign before the crowds get here," said Polly.

Everyone helped hang the sign in the window.

"I'm so excited!" said Shani. "Our pet talent show is going to be a huge hit!"

"There's only one problem," said Lila.

"What's that?" asked Polly.

"Cupcake. I can't teach her any tricks. All she wants to do is sleep!"

"No prob!" said Polly. "Cupcake is the perfect model for our salon services. People will come just to see her chillin' in the window."

Ollie spotted Snarls. He raced to the door and barked, just as Beth pulled him out of sight.

"Snarls, sit!" she hissed. "The pet show is going to be huge, all right," she said to Tori and Evie. "It's going to be a huge disaster! And I've called the television station to film the whole mess!"

"Oh, Beth," said Tori, "you think of everything!"

Beth grinned slyly and patted her backpack. "As Polly says, perfect planning is the key!"

By noon a supersized crowd had gathered in Polly's Fabulous Pet Palace, waiting for the show to begin.

"I hope the animals remember their tricks," whispered Lea.

Rick smiled. "Don't worry. Polly has planned everything perfectly."

Polly stepped up in front of the crowd. "Welcome to Polly's Fabulous Pet Palace. The show is now on!"

Shani gave Rainbow the thumbs-up signal to begin.

"I love coffee, I love tea," Rainbow began, hopping from one foot to the other as if he were jumping rope. "A, B, C, D, E, F, G!"

At that moment, an enormous purple grape came flying through the air.

"Perfect aim," whispered Beth, hidden in the crowd.

"Way to go!" Evie said.

The grape sailed past Rainbow and hit Cupcake on the head. Rainbow gave a loud squawk and swooped down to grab the grape. Startled, Cupcake jumped to her feet, tipping over Kicker's cage. The hamster scurried out and raced through the store with Cupcake close behind.

"Cupcake come back here!" shouted Lila.

Ollie barked excitedly.

"We have to stop them!" cried Polly.

Beth grinned. "This is even better than I planned."

Rainbow gulped down the grape and jumped on Kicker's wheel.

"A lemon, a lime, you better be on time when the school bell rings at quarter to nine!" he sang, spinning faster and faster.

The crowd roared with laughter. Kicker scurried up one end of the seesaw in the pet playground. Cupcake leaped on the other end, sending the hamster flying up to Rainbow's perch, where he clung, terrified.

"Hang on, Kicker!" yelled Rick.

Kicker hung on for a moment before diving into a bag of dog food.

"Cheee! Cheee!" scolded Hopscotch, jumping up and down.

"Whee! Yippee! Look at me! A, B, C, D, E, F, G!" sang Rainbow, skating down a slide and into the puppy pool with a big splash. The crowd cheered.

Hopscotch leaped up to an overhead rafter and swung from his tail. The children in the crowd shrieked with laughter.

"Cheee! Choo-choo-choo!" trilled the monkey, enjoying the attention. He dropped down to a shelf, tipping over a box of dazzling pet jewels. A tiny, gold crown spun through the air, landing right on top of Rainbow's head!

The crowd exploded into applause. Everyone was
cheering and shouting.

"This is the most amazing pet show I've ever seen!"

"Totally unbelievable!"

"And we've captured the whole thing for our TV show!"
said a man, stepping forward.

Polly noticed a television crew standing nearby with cameras. Her face fell. "You mean our pet show is going to be on TV? But it's a major—" "—Masterpiece!" finished the man. "And you are on TV, right now, live!"

Polly and her friends jumped up and down.

"Wow!"

"I can't believe it!"

"I must be dreaming!"

In the crowd, Snarls grabbed half of a hot dog someone had dropped and slunk off to eat it.

"Poor Snarls!" said Evie. "He didn't get to be top dog after all."

"Not yet!" snapped Beth. "But wait until next time. He'll come out on top, and so will I!"

The producer of the television show stepped forward.

"There's just one question I'd like to ask," she said, holding the microphone up to Polly. "How did you ever manage to stage such a fabulous pet show?"

Rainbow flew onto Shani's shoulder.

"I love coffee, I love tea!" he chanted. "Perfect planning is the key!"

Meet Polly and her friends!

Polly

Lea

Shani

Rick

polly pocket™

Lila